Tom and the Enchanted Flute

by Jean Gilder

© THE MEDICI SOCIETY LTD · LONDON 1985.   Printed in England.   B80.   ISBN 0 85503 080 1

Tom Badger lay on his tummy in the sun. He was reading *Woodland Antics* which was his favourite comic. Suddenly a hail of acorns rained down on him, hurting his head and landing with a 'whack' on his magazine.

He knew who it was and jumped up with an angry shout. 'Go away, Catkin, I know you're up there!'

Tom stared into the Oak tree, but he couldn't see Catkin squirrel.

As Tom started to walk home he met his friend Woody Mole, who was crying. 'Whatever's the matter, Woody?' he enquired. 'It's that beastly Thistle Hedgehog, he bumped into me on purpose, and he's so prickly!' 'Never mind, Woody,' said Tom, 'Here are some dock leaves to put on where it hurts.'

Tom was very kind, and soon Woody's tears dried up, and he trotted home happily.

Tom walked along with his head down, thinking. That gang was up to mischief again. There were Catkin Squirrel, Thistle Hedgehog, Albert the Magpie and Primrose Rabbit. Everywhere they went they meant trouble.

Mrs Rabbit's pegs were missing from the clothes line, Milly Dormouse's supply of hazel nuts was not to be found – Tom felt sure Albert had flown away with them.

Primrose was very silly, too, Tom thought. She would run up to a small friend and tweak her fur spitefully, then run away laughing. These four naughty creatures were making the village folk angry and miserable — what could he do?

Tom thought he would go and see his friend, Mr Chippy. Mr Chippy was very old and lived in a cosy house in the woods. Tom Badger knocked on his door, and Mr Chippy was delighted to see him.

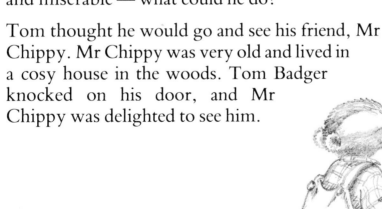

'Why, come on in, Tom,' he exclaimed cheerfully, 'Take a glass of blackberry wine with me.' Mr Chippy was very fond of his friend. He had taken a special interest in the Badger since he was small, as the stripes on his face were white on black, instead of the other way round.

Tom and Mr Chippy had a chat and exchanged news, then Tom told his friend about the four troublesome young animals. 'I don't know what to do, Tom,' said Mr Chippy thoughtfully, 'but I know who might be able to help!' He then told Tom to go and see a very wise old owl who lived in the witch tree, across the river.

'It's difficult to get to the other side.' said Mr Chippy, 'but you can use my boat, which I keep moored under the bank by the willow tree.' Tom thanked Mr Chippy, and said goodbye. As he turned to wave, Mr. Chippy called after him, 'you'll have to go at night — the wise owl sleeps all day and doesn't like being disturbed!'

Tom Badger decided to go that very night. There was a big moon and the wind chased the clouds across the sky.

He found the small boat tied up under the river bank as Mr Chippy had said. Tom climbed into the boat and started to row to the other side. The water looked dark and forbidding, and he felt rather frightened. It was hard work rowing against the fast flowing river.

Eventually he landed, much to his relief, and finding a root, secured the boat to it with a rope. Tom looked up into the strange, gnarled old tree, full of bristling branches. He walked all round the tree, but could see no way in.

'Hallo?' he called in a quavery voice, 'is anyone there?'

Then lights appeared up the tree, which showed a stairway winding up between the branches. Tom climbed this until he came to a small wooden door, which he knocked on, then opened.

'Mr Owl, are you there?' he called.
'Whoo – Whoo?'
'It's me, Tom Badger!'
'Whoo — Whoo.'
'I said, it's me, Tom . . .'
'I know, I know, don't shout!' said an irritable voice, 'Come in and don't hang about and let the draught in!'

Tom giggled nervously and stepped into the strangest room he had ever seen. It was dim and full of dusty books. There was a map of the stars and a telescope pointing out of a knot hole at the moon.

'Well, don't stand there staring, what is it you want?' snapped Owl. Tom explained about the troublesome gang, and Owl was so long in thought about this that Tom shuffled his feet and coughed, thinking Owl had gone to sleep.

'Shh,' said Owl fiercely, opening an eye and glaring at him. 'How can I think?'

Tom sat still for so long he fell asleep. 'Well, well, that's settled then,' came Owl's voice. 'Off you go, home now.'

Tom awakened with a start, and found he was being hustled out by an impatient Owl. 'But, you haven't told me . . .' began Tom.

Owl shuffled along the branch and said in a croaky voice:

'Those who need help
from troubles rare. . .
will find a few notes
will banish care!'

Then he swooped silently off into the night.

Tom felt puzzled. But when he arrived back at the boat there was a queer thin parcel on the seat, with a note 'For Tom, only use me if you must.' He unwrapped this excitedly and found it was a beautiful bamboo flute.

When Tom at last arrived home, very tired, he fell into bed clasping the flute and was soon asleep.

The next day Tom decided to go for a walk in the woods. After a while he sat down on a log. 'I don't know what to do,' he said to a robin perched on a nearby branch, 'so I shall play my flute.' He put the flute to his lips and blew gently.

A beautiful tune floated softly on the breeze and started the robin singing. After Tom stopped playing, the bushes nearby rustled and out stepped the gang! — Albert, Primrose, Thistle and Catkin.

'Oh, here's trouble,' groaned Tom — but they just sat down quietly and looked at him. 'Play your flute again, Tom,' they begged. So Tom played again and they listened entranced.

'Now,' said Tom, 'Why do you do so many naughty things, and upset everybody?'

'Because we are so bored,' said Catkin, twitching her tail.

'We want to be noticed,' remarked Albert.

'We *like* being naughty,' added Primrose and Thistle together.

'Nobody likes the things you do,' said Tom, 'it causes so much trouble'. Albert, where are Milly Dormouse's nuts, and Mrs Rabbit's pegs?' 'Caw,' squawked Albert, 'How did you know? They're in my nest actually,' he added, looking at his feet.

Tom sighed in despair; if only they had something to do. Then an idea came into his head, like a beam of sunshine.

'Oh, I know, let's put on a show!' he cried. 'A SHOW?' chorused the gang together. 'Yes!' said Tom, 'Primrose, I know you can dance! Catkin can be an acrobat, Thistle and Albert can be clowns!'

The gang looked at each other in astonishment. 'That would be fun,' said Catkin. 'We would be noticed, too,' added Albert.

'Righto, let's make costumes, and practise and practise,' said Tom joyfully. So Tom went to a jumble sale and bought some bright clothes, which they altered to make lovely outfits for the show.

'Have you noticed,' remarked Mrs Rabbit to Mrs Mole, 'The gang haven't been bothering us for days now — isn't it nice and peaceful?'

They saw a notice pinned on the oak tree. 'It says there is to be a *show* tonight — put on by the *GANG!* Would you believe it?' 'I'm not going, it's sure to be a trick!' said Mrs Rabbit firmly.

Meanwhile in a clearing in the woods, the gang and Tom were very busy. Curtains were drawn across the stage and seats lined up in front. Glow-worm lanterns were lit. Make-up and costumes were adjusted and the five animals waited eagerly for the audience to arrive.

The time came for the show to start. Albert, with the cord in his beak, was waiting to pull aside the curtain.

'Not yet,' said Tom, 'Nobody has come!' 'Oh dear!' Primrose burst out crying. 'That's because they don't trust us! Oh, I wish we hadn't been so naughty!'

Tom decided to play his flute again. As the beautiful music flowed out, the villagers began to gather to listen, entranced, by the flute.

When Tom finished playing, the whole village was there. He stood up and said 'Will you please stay for a little while? The gang have something to say to you.'

Albert hopped up and ruffled his wing feathers nervously, 'I'm sorry I pinched your pegs, Mrs Rabbit: and that I took your nuts, Milly! I will bring them back in the morning!' Then Primrose, Catkin and Thistle said they were sorry they had upset everybody. 'We will try not to be naughty, and will you watch our show, please?'

The village folk murmured in surprise and looked at each other. The gang held their breath, wondering if everybody would get up and go.

But then there were nods and smiles, and everybody clapped! So the show began.

What fun it was! Thistle Hedgehog and Albert in clown outfits did such funny things that everyone fell about laughing. Catkin did some very clever balancing acts, swinging upside down, so that everyone gasped in amazement.

Then Primrose danced gracefully while Tom played the flute, which was admired very much. Everyone agreed it was a marvellous show, and that the gang were very good. 'We will do a show again, soon,' said Tom. 'And that means we will be too busy to be naughty!' added Catkin. 'Well, *nearly* always!' said Thistle, and everyone laughed. As for wise old Owl, he looked at the stars through his telescope, knowing that, at last, all was well in the village.